The Grosset & Dunlap Read Aloud Library

Favorite Tales from Many Lands

Favorite

Publishers • GROSSET & DUNLAP • New York

Tales from Many Lands

Retold by Walter Retan

Illustrated by Linda Medley

A member of The Putnam Publishing Group

Text copyright © 1989 by Walter Retan. Illustrations copyright © 1989 by Linda Medley.
All rights reserved. Published by Grosset & Dunlap, Inc.,
a member of The Putnam Publishing Group, New York.
Published simultaneously in Canada. Printed and bound in Singapore.
Library of Congress Catalog Card Number: 87-83482 ISBN 0-448-19183-0
A B C D E F G H I J

Contents

Norway • The Three Billy Goats Gruff • 7

Spain • Little Half-Chick • 12

India • Tit for Tat • 21

Germany • The Wolf and the Seven Little Kids • 24

Russia • The Little Snow Maiden • 33

Rumania • Why the Woodpecker Has a Long Beak • 40

Japan • Little Peachling • 45

England • Lazy Jack • 52

France • The Three Wishes • 58

Central Africa • Why Cat and Rat Are No Longer Friends • 65

North America • The Eagles of Lost Opportunity • 72

Mexico • The Boy Who Made a Snake • 81

China • The Wonderful Pear Tree • 88

West Africa • How There Came To Be Anansi Stories • 94

The Three Billy Goats Gruff
Norway

Once upon a time there were three Billy Goats Gruff who lived together on a rocky Norwegian mountainside. There was very little food where the three goats lived, but across a deep valley they could see a pasture of tall, green grass. Every day they looked longingly at the pasture, and every day they wished that they could have some of that tall, green grass.

But to reach the pasture the three Billy Goats Gruff had to cross a wooden bridge. Under this bridge lived a great ugly troll, with eyes as big as saucers. The three Billy Goats Gruff were afraid of him.

One day the three billy goats were so hungry they decided they were going to cross the bridge, troll or no troll. The littlest Billy Goat Gruff crossed first.

Trip, trap! Trip, trap! went the bridge, as the goat's tiny hoofs hit the wooden planks.

"Who's that tripping over my bridge?" roared the fierce old troll.

"Oh, it is only I, the smallest Billy Goat Gruff," answered the goat in a soft little voice. "I am going across to the pasture to make myself fat."

"That is what *you* think!" roared the troll. "I am coming to gobble you up."

"Oh, no! Please don't do that," said the smallest billy goat. "I am too little to make a good meal for you. Wait for my brother, the second Billy Goat Gruff. He is much bigger than I am."

"Well, be off with you then," said the troll, licking his lips as he thought of the good meal he was going to have.

Soon the second Billy Goat Gruff came across the bridge.

TRIP, TRAP! TRIP, TRAP! TRIP, TRAP!

"Who's that tripping over my bridge?" roared the troll.

"Oh, it is only I, the second Billy Goat Gruff. I am going over to the pasture to make myself fat," answered the medium-sized billy goat, who did not have such a small voice.

"That is what *you* think!" roared the troll. "I am coming to gobble you up."

"Oh, no! Please don't do that," said the second Billy Goat Gruff. "You will have a better meal if you wait for my brother, the third Billy Goat Gruff. He's much, much bigger than I."

"Well, be off with you then," said the troll. His eyes glowed like live coals as he thought of the delicious meal he was going to have.

Just then, up came the big Billy Goat Gruff. TRIP, TRAP! TRIP, TRAP! TRIP, TRAP! went the bridge. The third Billy Goat Gruff was so heavy that the wooden planks shook and groaned.

"Who's that tramping and stamping over my bridge?" roared the troll.

"It is I, the biggest Billy Goat Gruff," answered the third brother, who had an ugly, hoarse voice of his own.

"Aha! I have been waiting for you!" roared the troll. "I am coming to gobble you up."

"That is what *you* think," answered the third Billy Goat Gruff.

As the wicked old troll climbed onto the bridge, the biggest Billy Goat Gruff lowered his horns and charged at the troll, knocking him right off the bridge. Down, down flew the old troll into the rushing stream of water at the bottom of the valley.

The third Billy Goat Gruff joined his two brothers in the pasture, where they all ate so much sweet green grass that they could scarcely walk back home.

Never again were they afraid to cross the bridge to the pasture.

Little Half-Chick
Spain

Long ago a fine, black Spanish hen hatched a brood of chicks. They were all pretty, plump little birds except for the youngest. When that one chipped his way out of his shell, his mother could scarcely believe her eyes. Instead of being a fluffy, soft little chick like the others, he looked as if he had been cut out of cardboard. He had only one leg, one wing, and one eye, and half a head and half a beak.

"Why, he is only half a chick," the mother hen said sadly. "He will never grow into a tall, handsome bird like the others. I will always have to keep him by my side so I can look after him."

But though Half-Chick looked queer and helpless, he was livelier than all the other chicks combined. When the family went for a stroll, Half-Chick always hopped off by himself and hid among the wheat stalks. When the mother hen clucked, the other chicks always came running, but Half-Chick pretended he could not hear because he had only one ear.

As he grew older, Half-Chick became even naughtier. He paid no attention to his poor mother, and he pecked at the other chicks for no reason at all.

One day he strutted up to his mother with his peculiar little hop and kick, and cocked his eye at her in a very bold way.

"Mother," he said, "I am tired of this boring farmyard. There is nothing here to see or do. I have decided to go to Madrid to visit the king."

"To Madrid!" his mother exclaimed. "Why, Half-Chick, whatever will you do in a big city like Madrid? And how do you expect to make such a long trip, hopping on one leg? You would be better off staying here with me."

But Half-Chick had made up his mind. Without even saying a proper good-by, he went off, hoppity-kick, down the high road that led to Madrid.

Later that day, as he was taking a shortcut through a field, he came to a stream. It was so overgrown with weeds and plants that its water could not flow freely.

"Oh, little Half-Chick," called the stream. "Do help me by clearing away these weeds."

"Help you, indeed!" exclaimed Half-Chick. "Don't you know I am on my way to Madrid to see the king? I have no time for such as you."

Hoppity-kick, hoppity-kick, away he stumped.

A little later he came to a campfire. It was burning low and would soon be out.

"Oh, little Half-Chick," called the fire. "Will you please put some sticks and dry leaves on me? Unless you help, I shall soon die."

"Help you, indeed!" exclaimed Half-Chick. "You can gather your own sticks. I am on my way to Madrid to see the king. I have no time for such as you."

The next morning Half-Chick came to a wide, paved road that he was sure must lead to Madrid. Beside the road stood a tall chestnut tree, and somehow the wind had gotten tangled in its branches.

"Oh, little Half-Chick," called the wind. "Do help me. If you would just hop up here and untangle me from these branches, I would be so grateful."

"Help you, indeed!" exclaimed Half-Chick. "Don't you know I am on my way to Madrid to see the king? It's your own fault you got caught in the tree. You can just get yourself out."

Away stumped Half-Chick, hopping faster and faster as the towers and roofs of Madrid came into view. At last he came to the king's palace. He was hopping past one of the kitchen windows when the cook saw him.

"There is the very thing I need," said the cook. "The king says that he wants to have chicken soup for his lunch."

Opening the window, the cook grabbed little Half-Chick and popped him into the broth pot. Poor little Half-Chick! The cold water covered his head and made his feathers stick to his sides.

"Water, water!" cried Half-Chick in terror. "Do have pity on me and stop wetting me like this."

"Ah, little Half-Chick," answered the water. "You would not help me when I was a stream clogged by plants. Now you must be punished."

Then the water began to boil. Half-Chick hopped from one side of the pot to the other, trying to get away from the heat.

"Fire, fire!" cried Half-Chick. "Do not scorch me like this. You are hurting me."

"Ah, little Half-Chick," replied the fire. "You refused to help me when I was dying in the woods. Now you must be punished."

Just as Half-Chick thought that he would surely die, the cook lifted the lid from the pot.

"Gracious me!" he exclaimed. "What is this thing I have put into the pot? I can't serve a queer creature like this to the king."

Lifting Half-Chick out of the pot with a big spoon, the cook threw him out the window. Suddenly the wind caught him and began to whirl him through the air. The poor chick could scarcely breathe.

"Oh, wind," he finally managed to gasp, "if you whirl me through the air like this, you will surely kill me."

"Ah, little Half-Chick," answered the wind. "When I was caught in the branches of the chestnut tree, you would not help me. Now you must be punished." And the wind whirled him away faster than ever till they reached the tallest church in the city. There the wind left Half-Chick fastened to the top of the steeple.

And there stands Half-Chick to this very day, perched on his one leg, gazing out over the city with his one eye. When the wind blows, Half-Chick creaks and turns. Sometimes he seems to be whispering, "Oh, dear, I should have been a better Half-Chick."

Tit for Tat
India

A camel and a jackal once lived near to each other in the south of India. Though they were an odd-looking pair, they became very good friends.

One day the jackal said to the camel, "I know a field where the sugarcane grows thick and sweet. If you like, I will show you where it is."

"By all means take me there," replied the camel. "I like nothing better than a good mess of sugarcane."

"There is just one problem," said the jackal. "The field is on the other side of the river, and I cannot swim. You will have to carry me across on your back."

"Gladly," said the camel.

So the jackal climbed onto the camel's back, and together they swam across the river. When they reached the other side, the jackal pointed out the sugarcane field. It was quite a distance from the shore.

"While you are eating sugarcane," he told the camel, "I will feast on the fish and crabs which are plentiful along the riverbank."

So the camel ambled slowly along toward the sugarcane, while the jackal ran up and down the shore eating bits of fish and a very large number of crabs.

Because jackals are much smaller than camels, he had eaten his fill by the time the camel reached the field of delicious sugarcane. His stomach could not hold another thing. He began to run up and down the riverbank, howling as loudly as he could.

When the villagers who lived nearby heard the jackal howling, they said, "Just listen to that jackal. We had better chase him away before he tears up all our plants and makes holes in the ground."

Carrying big sticks and stout branches, they rushed to the sugarcane field. To their astonishment, they found a camel standing there alone, chewing stalks of their precious sugarcane. They forgot about the jackal and began hitting the camel instead. The poor creature had barely enough strength to flee to the river.

No sooner had the camel reached the riverbank than the noisy jackal jumped up on the camel's back, shouting, "Hurry! Get us across the water before those villagers catch us."

The camel swam as fast as he could until they had reached the deepest part of the river. Then he asked, "Tell me, my friend, why did you begin to howl as soon as you had eaten your fill? I had barely gotten started on the sugarcane when the villagers heard your howls and came rushing to the field. They beat me black and blue and nearly killed me with their big sticks."

"I really don't know," said the jackal. "It is just a habit of mine to start howling as soon as I have eaten my fill."

When the camel heard that, he began to roll this way and that in the water.

"What are you doing?" asked the terrified jackal. "Don't you know I can't swim?"

"It is just a habit of mine to start rolling over and over after I have been eating sugarcane," answered the camel.

At that, the camel rolled completely over on his back, shaking off the jackal as he did so. The foolish jackal drowned, but the camel swam safely back to the other side of the river.

The Wolf and the Seven Little Kids
Germany

Once upon a time a mother goat lived with her seven kids in a cozy little cottage at the edge of the forest.

One day the mother goat decided to go look for food for her family. Calling the seven little kids together, she said, "My dear children, while I am gone, be sure to stay inside with the door locked. And whatever you do, look out for that tricky old wolf. You can recognize the rascal by his gruff voice and black feet. If he gets in, he will surely eat you—skin, bones, and everything."

"Don't you worry, Mother," answered the seven little kids. "We'll be very careful. Never fear."

The mother goat kissed them all, then set off toward the forest.

Before long there came a knock on the door and a voice called out, "Open the door, children dear. It is your mother back with treats for all of you."

"You are not our mother," answered one of the little kids. "She has a pleasant, sweet voice. Your voice is gruff and loud."

"I think you are the wolf," said another little kid. "Go away and stop bothering us."

But the old rascal of a wolf wasn't to be put off so easily. He went home and drank a mixture of honey and syrup to make his voice gentle and sweet. Then he came knocking at the cottage door again.

"Who is it?" asked the seven little kids.

"It is your mother, dear children," answered the wolf in his new, honey-sweet voice. And, indeed, this time it did sound like their mother.

But suddenly one of the kids spied the wolf's paw on the windowsill. "You can't fool us, old wolf," he shouted. "We can see your hairy black paw. Our mother has pretty white paws."

Still the old wolf did not give up. He went to the baker and told him he had hurt his foot. The baker wrapped it with some sticky dough and sprinkled white flour all over it. Then the wolf ran back to the cottage.

Again he knocked at the door, calling out, "Let me in, children dear. This is your mother, home at last. I have brought a nice present for each of you."

When the seven kids heard the honey-sweet voice and spied the white paw on the windowsill, they were sure that their mother had come home at last. They opened the door wide.

To their horror, in rushed the fierce wolf. The terrified kids scattered in every direction. One scurried under the table. Another jumped into the bed. The third hid in the oven. The fourth shut himself in the closet, while the fifth got into the washtub. The sixth hid under the sink, and the seventh and smallest squeezed into the tall grandfather clock. But the wolf found them, one by one, and gobbled them down without even taking time to chew. The only one he missed was the smallest kid, who had hidden in the clock case.

Finally, his appetite satisfied, the wolf took himself off. But his stomach was so heavy that he did not walk far. He lay down in the nearby meadow and fell asleep.

Not long after, the mother goat came home. What a sight greeted her eyes! The table and chairs lay on their sides. The teapot had shattered into a hundred pieces, and somebody had ripped all the sheets and pillowcases from the beds.

One by one, she called the names of the seven little kids, but there was no answer until she came to the seventh and smallest.

A wee little voice cried out, "Here I am, Mother dear, hidden in the clock case."

When the little kid told her how the wolf had come and eaten all
the other kids, the poor mother goat began to weep and wail. But
suddenly she heard loud snores coming from outside. She and the
little kid went out to the meadow, where they found the wolf asleep
under a tree. They could see something moving around in his stomach.

"Quick!" said the mother to her kid. "Bring me my sewing
basket. Perhaps they are not yet dead."

Taking her scissors, she carefully cut a hole in the side of the wolf.
Out popped the head of one of the kids. Then—one after another—
all six kids jumped out. The greedy wolf had swallowed them whole!

It would be hard to know who was happier—the mother or her seven kids. But the wise mother goat knew there was no time to waste.

"Each of you must bring me a big stone right away," she said.

Quickly she took the stones and stuffed them into the wolf's stomach. Then she sewed him back up so he looked as good as new.

By the time the old wolf woke up, the mother goat and her kids had hidden themselves in the cottage. Feeling very thirsty after his feast, the old wolf waddled down to the stream to get a drink. With each step, the stones rattled and rolled about in his stomach. He could not imagine why six little kids should make such a racket.

When the wolf finally reached the stream, he leaned over to take a drink. But the stones in his stomach were so heavy that he fell into the water with a great splash and drowned.

The seven little kids, watching from the window, came running out of the cottage. "The wolf is dead! The wolf is dead!" they shouted. Together with their mother they danced around the meadow with joy.

Never again did they open the door without being absolutely sure who was standing outside.

The Little Snow Maiden
Russia

Long ago, in Russia, there lived a peasant named Ivan, who had been married for many years to his wife, Marousha. The couple had never had any children, and this made them very sad. They spent many hours at the window of their small house, watching the children of the village play together.

"If only heaven had seen fit to bless us by sending us a child of our own," said the old man with a sigh.

"Alas, my good husband," replied Marousha, "what is not to be is not to be. Let us be thankful for each other."

Then one winter day there was a big snowstorm—and what a storm it was! By the time the flakes stopped falling, the snow was so deep it reached to the knees of the tallest man in the village.

The children rushed out of their houses, dressed in their warmest jackets and gloves, and set to work building a big snowman.

Ivan and his wife were watching as usual from their window, when Ivan suddenly said, "Good wife, why should we not go out and build our own snowman?"

"Better yet," replied Marousha, "let us make a little snow doll. We can pretend it is our own living child."

The old couple went out into their garden and set to work. With great care they made a little body, then shaped two little hands and arms and two little legs and feet. On top they placed a ball of snow from which to carve out a head.

Next they shaped a nose and a chin, and dug out two holes for eyes. Then Ivan carefully hollowed out a mouth. No sooner had he finished this than he felt a warm breath on his cheek. Stepping back in surprise, he looked closely at the snow doll. Its eyes were now a sparkling blue. Its lips were curled up in a merry smile.

"What is this?" Ivan exclaimed. "Some sort of magic?"

The snow doll bent its head and moved its little arms and legs just as if it were alive.

"Ivan! Ivan!" exclaimed Marousha. "We have a child at last—our own little girl." The old woman knelt down in front of the little snow maiden and kissed her.

They led the little doll into the house, where she began to grow bigger—hour by hour—until she was the size of a real little girl. Her hair was long and golden and her lips were bright red. As she laughed and chattered away, the little house was filled with a new kind of excitement and happiness.

The old couple loved their new daughter. Ivan told her stories and taught her songs to sing. Marousha sewed new dresses for her and taught her how to read and write. The little girl was very clever and learned everything quickly.

At mealtime she wanted nothing but ice chopped up into little bits like cereal. And, when inside, she always preferred to stay in a cool part of the house away from the fire.

All the children in the neighborhood came to play with the little snow maiden. She showed them how to build wonderful things out of snow and ice, and she was always kind to her new friends.

As the winter went on, Ivan and Marousha were so happy that they scarcely noticed when the days began to grow longer and the sun shone brighter, melting the snow. Soon little green stalks of grass pushed up through the last bits of ice, and songbirds once again flew high in the air.

Spring had come to the small village, and all the children gathered in the middle of the green to dance and sing and play games. Only the little snow maiden sat still and sad by the cottage window.

"What is the matter, child?" Marousha asked. "Why are you so sad?"

"It is nothing, Mother," answered the little girl.

But as the spring sun melted the last of the snow and the fields filled with flowers, the little snow maiden grew even sadder. She hid from her playmates and stayed curled up in the shadows.

Spring passed into summer, and one day the village girls came begging her to walk into the woods with them to search for wild flowers. Though the snow maiden did not wish to join them, Marousha said, "Go with your friends. They will take good care of you, and you will be happy in the shade of the tall trees."

The girls looked for wild flowers and ran among the trees. Everything the others did, the little snow maiden did, too. Then, as the sun began to set, the girls lit a fire of dry grass and lined up in a row, with the little snow maiden at the end.

"Watch us!" they shouted. "And do just as we do." One after another they ran toward the fire and jumped over it with a big leap.

The last girl to cross the fire heard a soft sigh behind her. Then came another sound like the sizzling of cold water in a hot frying pan. But when she turned to see what had made the noise, she found nothing behind her.

What had happened to the little snow maiden?

Perhaps she has hidden from us to play a joke, the girls thought. But though they searched behind every tree, and called to her over and over again, they found no trace of the little snow maiden.

Deciding that she must have gone home, they returned to the village. But they didn't find her there, either. For many days Ivan and Marousha searched everywhere, but they did not find their little daughter. Alas, when the first breath of flame touched her as she jumped over the fire, she had simply melted away.

One day, as the autumn winds were blowing colder, Marousha sat
staring out the window at the garden where the little snow maiden
had played.

"When winter comes again," she said, "we can make another snow
doll. If heaven is kind, perhaps she will once more come to life."

Ivan turned to Marousha and nodded. The old couple smiled at the
happy thought.

Why the Woodpecker Has a Long Beak
Rumania

Once upon a time there lived an old lady who could never mind her own business. She went from one house to another, sticking her long, sharp nose into her neighbors' pots and pans, peering into their cupboards, and peeking under their beds.

She was always carrying tales from one person to another. But since her ears were neither as long nor as sharp as her nose, she seldom got her facts right. So she created no end of mischief among her neighbors, who heartily wished she would take herself and her long nose elsewhere.

One day the old lady was walking through the woods, sticking her long nose around first one tree and then another. Suddenly, a tall man dressed in black appeared before her. In his hand he carried a huge sack, tightly tied with a long piece of rope. The old woman spied the sack at once, and her long nose began to sniff and twitch and poke around it.

"Old woman, this sack is for you," said the man. "I want you to carry it home. Keep it beside you at all times but never, never put your nose inside it. If you let your curiosity get the better of you, you will find more than you bargain for. Worse, you will have troubles without end."

"Heaven forbid!" replied the old lady. "I would never peek inside. I have no curiosity whatsoever about the contents of this sack."

Immediately, she flung the sack over her shoulder and hobbled off toward home. Already her fingers were twitching, so eager was she to get into the bag. She had heard tales of fairy folk who lived in the woods and gave mortals wonderful gifts of gold and silver and precious jewels.

As soon as the old lady got out of the woods, she sat down in the middle of a field and opened the sack. But what a surprise! Out scrambled a wriggling mass of beetles, midges, ants, and other insects. Away they scampered, each one running in a different direction as fast as its little legs would take it. Some hid in the earth, others scrabbled under grass, and many crawled up into trees.

When the old woman saw what had happened, she nearly died from fright. Running frantically to and fro, she tried to catch the little insects and stuff them back into the sack. But most of them were too fast and too smart for her. She was about to give up and head for home when the strange man from the woods appeared again.

"Is this the way you honor my request?" he asked. He looked at her sternly. "Where are all the midges and ants and beetles that were in the sack? Because your curiosity caused you to stick your nose into my sack, you must take the consequences. From this moment on, you shall become a bird and go about picking up all the insects you have let loose. Only when the sack is completely filled again, will you once more become a human being."

By the time he finished speaking, the old woman had indeed turned into a woodpecker. Her very long nose had become a long woodpecker's beak. To this day she goes about hunting for beetles and midges and ants, hoping to get them all back into the bag so that she will regain her human form. But since she has never come close to completing her task, she remains a woodpecker, endlessly tapping on trees with her long beak, forever searching for insects.

Little Peachling
Japan

Many hundreds of years ago, in far-off Japan, there lived an old woodcutter and his wife. They were poor people who lived alone in a small farmhouse, for they had never been blessed with any children.

One bright summer morning the old woodcutter went off to the hills as usual to gather firewood. His wife walked down to the river to wash clothes. While she was scrubbing her laundry in the fresh, clear water, what should she see but a huge peach floating down the stream toward her. Truly she had never seen such a large, beautiful-looking peach in her entire life.

Using a long bamboo branch, she managed to pull the peach out of the water. Though it was very heavy, she loaded the peach into her laundry basket, which she carried home on her back.

"What a treat that peach will be for my good husband," she said.

Soon afterward the old woodcutter came down from the hills. When his wife placed the peach on the table before him, he marveled at its rosy redness and amazing size. But just as he picked up his long, sharp knife to cut the peach in halves, the fruit split in two. In the very center, where the pit should have been, lay a tiny, perfectly shaped baby boy. Immediately, the little boy jumped to his feet and started running around the tabletop.

"Goodness me!" exclaimed the old man. "Did you ever?" said the old woman. They were both delighted with the tiny child and treated him as if he were their own son, calling him *Momotaro*—Little Peachling.

The years passed and Little Peachling grew up to be strong and brave. On the day of his fifteenth birthday, he came to his parents and said, "You have been very kind to me. Now it is time I did something in return. I am going off to the island of the ogres to put an end to their evil mischief-making and bring back the treasure they have stolen. All I ask is that you kindly make some of your delicious millet dumplings for my journey."

The old woodcutter ground some millet, and his wife baked a batch of dumplings. Little Peachling put them in a wallet, which he fastened to the girdle he wore around his waist. Then, bidding his parents good-by, he set off cheerfully on his adventure.

"*Sayonara,*" cried the old man and woman, as Little Peachling disappeared down the path.

He had not gone far before he met a monkey.

"*Kia! Kia!*" gibbered the monkey. "Where are you going, Little Peachling?"

"I am going to the island of the ogres to put an end to their mischief-making," said Little Peachling.

"What is that I see fastened to your girdle?" asked the monkey.

"I am carrying some of the best millet dumplings in all Japan," answered Little Peachling.

"If you will give me one, I will travel with you," said the monkey.

Little Peachling pulled out a dumpling and gave it to the monkey, who followed along behind.

When they had gone a little farther, they met a pheasant with feathers of many brilliant colors.

"*Ken! Ken!*" said the pheasant. "Where are you going, Little Peachling?"

"I am going to the island of the ogres to carry away their stolen treasure," answered Little Peachling.

"What is that I see fastened to your girdle?" asked the pheasant.

"I am carrying some of the best millet dumplings in all Japan," answered Little Peachling.

"If you will give me one, I will go with you," said the pheasant.

So Little Peachling pulled out another dumpling and gave it to the pheasant.

When the three travelers had gone a little farther, they met a dog.

"*Bow-wow!*" said the dog. "Where are you going, Little Peachling?"

"I am going to the island of the ogres to put an end to their mischief-making and carry away their stolen treasure," answered Little Peachling.

"If you will just give me one of those nice millet dumplings I can smell in your girdle, I will go with you," said the dog.

"Most willingly," answered Little Peachling, handing him a dumpling. He continued on his way with the monkey, the pheasant, and the dog following along.

When the four friends arrived at the seashore, they found a small boat. Boarding it, they sailed to the island of the ogres.

"Now listen carefully to my plan," said Little Peachling. "Pheasant, you must fly over the castle wall and peck at the eyes of the ogres. Monkey, you clamber over the castle wall and unlock the gate from the inside. Then go after the ogres, pinching and scratching them. Dog and I will rush in through the gate. Dog will bite the ogres while I take after them with my sword."

And that is just what they did. Though the wicked ogres fought fiercely, they had been taken by surprise. Little Peachling and his friends quickly put them to flight.

"And now," said Little Peachling, "let us look for the ogres' treasure."

What a treasure it proved to be! There were caps and coats that made their wearers invisible. There were heaps of gold and silver and big chests filled with precious jewels.

The four friends carried the treasure back to the mainland in their boat. Then they packed it into a cart, and pulled the cart all the way back to the house where the old woodcutter and his wife lived.

The treasure enabled the old couple, as well as their neighbors, to live in peace and plenty for the rest of their lives. As for Little Peachling and his three friends, they became great heroes throughout the countryside. Never again was anybody troubled by the wicked, mischief-making ogres.

Lazy Jack
England

There was once a boy named Jack who lived with his mother in a tiny English cottage. The poor old woman earned a little money by spinning, but Jack sat around all day doing nothing at all. The neighbors called him Lazy Jack.

Finally his mother had enough of Jack's laziness. She told him he would have to work for his porridge or find another place to live.

The very next morning Jack hired himself to a farmer for a penny. At the end of the day he proudly headed home, carrying his penny. But since he had never had any money before, he didn't know how to take care of it. He dropped it into a brook and couldn't find it again.

"Oh, you silly boy," said his mother when she learned what had happened. "You should have put it in your pocket."

"Indeed I should have," said Jack. "Another time I'll do so."

The next morning Jack hired himself to a cow keeper, who gave him a jar of fresh milk for his day's work. This time Jack carefully put the jar into one of his pockets. Of course the milk slopped all over, so there was nothing left by the time he got home.

"Oh, you clumsy fellow," said his mother. "Don't you know you should have carried it on your head?"

"Indeed I should have," Jack replied. "Another time I'll do so."

The next day Jack hired himself to another farmer, who gave him a big, creamy cheese for his labor. Jack carefully placed the cheese under his hat. But on the way home the cheese melted, sticking to his hair and running down his face.

"Oh, you foolish boy," said his mother when she saw the spoiled cheese. "You should have carried it in your hands."

"Indeed I should have," said Jack. "Another time I'll do so."

In the morning Jack hired himself to a baker. The baker was a mean fellow who gave Jack nothing but a big, gray tomcat for his work. Jack tried to carry the cat in his hands, but the cat hated being picked up. It scratched Jack so badly that he had to let it go.

"Dear me," said his mother when she heard what had happened. "Don't you know you should have tied it with a string and pulled it along behind you?"

"Indeed I should have," said Jack. "Another time I'll do so."

The next day Jack hired himself to a butcher, who gave Jack a big ham for his day's work. Remembering his mother's advice, Jack tied a string to the ham and dragged it along behind him. By the time he got home, the ham was ruined.

"Oh, you nincompoop!" said his mother. "Now we won't have anything but cabbage for our Sunday dinner. You should have carried the ham on your shoulder."

"Indeed I should have," Jack agreed. "Another time I'll do so."

In the morning Jack hired himself to a donkey herder, who gave him a donkey in return for his hard work. Jack had quite a time getting the donkey onto his shoulders, but at last he succeeded.

Now it happened that along the way to Jack's cottage, there lived a rich man with his only daughter. She was a beautiful girl, but she had never spoken in her whole life. The doctors said she wouldn't be able to speak until somebody made her laugh.

The maiden was looking out the window on the very day that Jack

staggered past with the donkey. The poor animal was braying with all its strength, and its four legs were sticking out in the air.

The sight was so comical that the girl burst out into a great fit of laughter and ran outside, shouting to her father to come look at the funny sight. Her father was so overjoyed to hear his daughter laugh and talk that he insisted that Jack marry her and live in his big house.

So Lazy Jack became a rich gentleman. As for his mother, the astonished old woman lived with the happy couple until she died.

The Three Wishes
France

There once lived a poor French woodcutter who had grown very tired of his hard life. Though he worked from morning to night, he never had much money or good food.

One day he was feeling more discouraged than ever. "Nothing seems to go right for me," he complained. "And nothing I have ever wished for has been granted to me."

Scarcely had he finished speaking when a little red-cheeked man with a green pointed cap appeared from behind a tree. The woodcutter was so surprised that he dropped his bundle of branches.

"Do not be afraid," said the little man. "I heard you talking and I have come to help. I promise that the first three wishes you make will be granted—whatever they may be. But you must think very hard about what you really want. Your happiness will depend on it."

At that, the little man vanished. The woodcutter was overjoyed. Throwing his bundle over his shoulder, he walked happily home.

"I must think carefully about these wishes," he told himself. "And I will ask my wife's opinion, too."

When he reached his little cottage he called out, "Fanny, I am home. Make a fire and prepare a hearty meal. I have good news."

While they ate, he told his wife what had happened. "Just think," he said, "we can be rich for life. We have only to make the right three wishes."

Fanny began to think of all sorts of extravagant ideas—jewels, castles, servants. . . . Anything was possible!

"Now, Fanny," the woodcutter warned her, "we must wish for nothing hastily. I think we should first get a good night's sleep. Then in the morning we can make our first wish."

"You are quite right, my dear husband," said his wife. "But first let me fetch the wine so we can celebrate our good fortune with a toast in front of the fireplace."

As the woodcutter sipped his wine, he stretched out in front of the blazing fire. "Ah, this is the life!" he exclaimed. "The wine is perfect. I just wish I had a good length of sausages to go with it."

No sooner had he spoken than a string of sausages fell down the chimney. Fanny let out a scream.

"Look at what you have done," she scolded. "You and your greed! You have wasted one of our precious wishes on nothing but a string of sausages to fill your stomach." The woodcutter tried to silence her, but on and on she went. Finally she told her poor husband that he was no better than a jackass to have made such a foolish wish.

At that, the woodcutter flew into a rage. "I have heard enough!" he shouted. "I wish those sausages were hanging from your nose."

Alas, no sooner had he spoken than the string of sausages fastened itself to Fanny's nose. No matter how much she pulled or how hard she tried to cut them off, the sausages remained stuck fast.

Now Fanny was a pretty woman, but the sausages dangling from her nose made her look very ugly indeed. Furthermore, they covered her mouth and prevented her from speaking. When her husband discovered that, he thought at first that he hadn't made such a bad wish after all. But then he began to think about what he had done.

"I have wasted two of my three wishes," he told himself. "I had better make the best possible use of the third. Perhaps I should wish to be a king. Then I would have a fine castle, jewels, servants, and plenty of gold."

But immediately he thought about his poor wife. "She would be queen," he thought. "But what a funny-looking queen, with a string of sausages hanging from her nose. Of course, if she *were* queen, nobody would dare tell her how funny she looked . . . "

The woodcutter thought and thought. He wasn't at all sure that he wanted to exchange his pretty wife for an ugly queen. Finally he decided that he should put the question to her. Would she rather be as pretty as she once was, or would she prefer to turn into a funny-looking queen? Without any hesitation, Fanny chose to have her own straight nose and go back to being a poor woodcutter's pretty wife.

So the woodcutter did not become a rich king with a castle and plenty of gold. Instead he used his last wish to turn his wife back into her old self.

And from that day on he was much happier, which shows that men are really not very good at making wishes—no matter how happy they think it will make them.

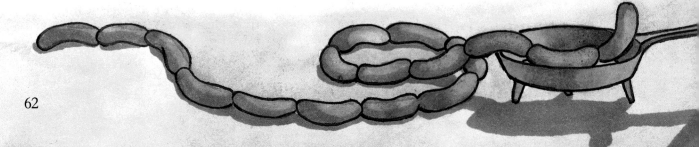

Why Cat and Rat Are No Longer Friends
Central Africa

There was a time—long, long ago—when Cat and Rat were good friends. They lived together on an island in Central Africa and led a very happy life. Cat climbed trees and hunted birds. Rat ate nuts and roots from the cassava trees.

But of course no one is ever quite satisfied. One day Rat said to Cat, "I am tired of living on this island, eating the same things day after day. We should find a village where *you* wouldn't have to hunt for birds all the time and *I* could get food without digging in the ground."

"A good idea!" said Cat. "But how do we get off this island? There is all that water to cross."

"Very simple," said Rat, who had been thinking. "We can carve a boat from a big cassava root."

No sooner said than done. Together they dug up an enormous cassava root. Rat gnawed and gnawed with his sharp teeth until there was a hollow in the root large enough to hold both of them. Cat, meanwhile, scratched and scratched until the outside was smooth and free of dirt.

After making two little paddles, they started on their journey across the great water. The trip was much longer than they had expected. By the time the sun rose high in the sky, they began to feel hungry. But because they had thought the journey would be short, they had not brought any food.

Cat curled up in one end of the boat and went to sleep. Rat decided to curl up in the other end and go to sleep, too. But hard as he tried, he couldn't stop thinking about how hungry he was.

Suddenly Rat had an idea! Since their boat was made from a cassava root, why couldn't he just take a few bites from the bottom?

So while Cat slept, Rat began to gnaw—*nibble, nibble, nibble.*

Finally the noise woke up Cat. "What is that noise?" she asked. But Rat shut his eyes and pretended to be sleeping.

Cat looked around. "I must have been dreaming," she said, and went back to sleep.

Rat began eating again—*nibble, nibble, nibble.*

"What is that noise?" Cat asked, waking up once more.

Again Rat pretended to be fast asleep.

"I must be having some strange dreams," said Cat.

And so it went. Rat would nibble. Cat would wake up. Rat would pretend to be asleep. Cat would go back to sleep.

But in his greed Rat finally nibbled so much that he made a hole in the bottom of the boat. Water began to leak in.

"What is going on?" shouted Cat, waking up and leaping onto one end of the boat.

"I cannot imagine," lied Rat.

But Cat knew better. "You are a wicked creature!" she cried. "You have been eating our boat."

"I was so hungry," squeaked Rat. But just then the boat began to sink and there was no more time for arguing. They had to swim for their lives.

"I am going to eat you," said Cat, glaring at Rat as she paddled through the water.

"Don't eat me now," said Rat. "You will get your mouth full of water and drown. Wait until we reach shore."

"I will wait," thought Cat to herself. "But the minute we reach shore, I will put a quick end to that villain."

As soon as their feet touched dry land, Cat leaped toward Rat, shouting, "Now I am going to eat you."

"I certainly deserve it," said Rat. "But wait until I dry myself. Then I will taste better."

So they sat down to dry in the bright sunlight. Cat got so interested in licking her fur, making it glossy and smooth again, that she didn't notice Rat digging a hole in front of a tall tree.

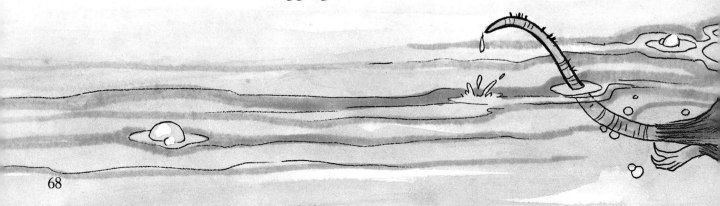

At last Cat finished grooming her coat. "Are you ready now?" she asked. "I am going to eat you—ready or not!"

"Of course I am ready," answered Rat, disappearing into his hole.

"You rascal!" Cat exclaimed when she saw the little hole, just big enough for Rat. "I hope you realize you will never get out of there alive. I am going to wait right here until you have to come out."

"I may never come out," answered Rat.

"Then you will starve," said Cat. She settled down beside the hole with her nose on her front paws and all four legs folded under her.

For the rest of the day Rat went on digging and digging, while Cat waited. By the time the sun had gone down, Rat had secretly dug a tunnel under the tree and up the other side. In the dark of night, he quietly crept out the other end and went into a nearby village.

When Cat discovered his trick, she was furious. And to this day she is never so sleepy that she doesn't hear the gnawing of a rat. Nor does she ever tire of watching for him to come out of his hole.

As for Rat, he knows he has to be careful. If there is a cat lurking anywhere near a house where he goes to steal food, she will be waiting for him. And she will never be satisfied until she manages to eat him for dinner.

This is why Cat and Rat are no longer friends.

The Eagles of Lost Opportunity

North America (Delaware Indian)

Ne-qua-la was a proud, young Indian brave. He walked with his head held high and his black eyes full of shining light.

One day Ne-qua-la decided that he should have a fine headdress of eagle feathers. "Let the other young braves pick up their feathers from the base of the cliffs where the eagles nest," he told himself. "I shall use only feathers plucked from the tails of live eagles."

Ne-qua-la set out for the high cliffs, stopping only long enough to kill a wolf in the middle of the deep woods. He took the wolf's flesh with him to use as bait.

Higher and higher Ne-qua-la climbed until white, fluffy clouds were drifting all around him. Finally he reached a bare peak on which grew one short, stunted pine tree. As the young brave looked down into the valley below, he saw hundreds of eagles circling lazily in and out among the hills.

"In a place like this," he told himself, "it will be easy to get the kind of feathers I want."

Hanging a big piece of wolf meat over the cliff, he hid behind the thick branches of the pine. In his hand, he held a long stick with a noose on the end. While the eagle was feeding, he would slip the noose over the bird's head and capture him.

Soon a beautiful eagle saw the bait and swooped down. Ne-qua-la's lips curled in scorn. "He is only a young bird," the brave said. "Not worth bothering with. Get away!" he shouted, waving his pole. "I am looking for much bigger feathers than you are wearing." The eagle screamed and flew away.

Almost at once Ne-qua-la heard the flapping of other wings. Over the tree darted a fine eagle, much larger than the first. But again the young brave's lips curled in disgust. "You, also, are too young," he cried. "You have no feathers big enough for *my* fine headdress." Again he jumped out and waved his pole, frightening the eagle away.

An hour passed before a third eagle caught sight of the wolf meat swinging in the wind. He flew up with a mighty rush of wings. Once more Ne-qua-la's lips curled in scorn. "You are big enough," he said, "but your feathers are not the color I want for my headdress. Get away before I beat you with my stick!"

The big eagle flew away, while Ne-qua-la complained about his bad luck. "Here I sit half a day without finding an eagle of the right size and color. Why can I not get what I want?" he asked.

Suddenly he heard a scream and felt a rush of air driven by mighty, beating wings. The sharp talons of a huge eagle gripped his shoulders tightly as Ne-qua-la felt himself lifted from the cliff. He was zooming through the clouds with the earth far, far below. Ahead loomed the steep side of the very highest peak, and on the top he spied a gigantic nest made of big fir trees. At that instant the talons let go of his shoulders, and he dropped down beside the huge nest.

"Fool!" shrieked the big eagle. "I, the ruler of the whole eagle tribe, sent three of my finest subjects to you. But you were so blinded by greed that you could not see how long and beautiful their feathers were. One after another, you let your opportunities pass by. Now, as a punishment for those lost opportunities, you must stay here in the cold and the wind, far away from your people. It will be your duty to tend the brood of young eaglets in this nest. If you tend them well, feeding and caring for them lovingly, one of them will no doubt grow strong enough to carry you back to the tepees of your tribe."

With a wild scream, the great eagle flew off, leaving Ne-qua-la beside the nest.

"Alas," said the brave, "the eagle spoke the truth. I was certainly blinded by my greed. Because I kept insisting on something better, I failed to take advantage of the opportunities that were offered to me."

It was cold and lonely there on the high peak. Poor Ne-qua-la had only the wind and the wild screams of the young eaglets to keep him company. But the young brave accepted his fate with good cheer and tended the brood with loving care. Before long they grew into handsome birds.

Once a week the great red mother eagle swept down with a deer for the eaglets to eat. "The eaglets are thriving under your care," she would say. "Hope grows bright for your release."

Finally the day arrived when the eaglets wanted to try their wings. "Be careful," warned Ne-qua-la, who had grown fond of his charges. "The earth is a long way below you."

"Do not fear," the eaglets replied. "Our wings are now strong and trustworthy."

One by one, the young birds hopped out of the huge nest and flew off the side of the cliff. When the last one had gone, Ne-qua-la sat on the edge of the nest, feeling sad.

"Alas," he said, "though I took good care of them, not one eaglet offered to carry me away from this place. Now I shall surely die from cold and starvation."

A week passed. Then one bright morning Ne-qua-la saw a mighty eagle speeding directly toward him.

"Ne-qua-la," cried the bird, as it circled the young brave's head, "do you not know me? I am one of the eaglets you tended so carefully and with such love."

"I cannot believe it," replied Ne-qua-la. "You have grown so big and handsome."

"All things must be little before they are great," said the bird. "Now I have come to carry you back to the valley."

A moment later Ne-qua-la stood safe at the foot of the cliffs. All around him were beautiful eagle feathers.

"Thank you," cried the young brave, as the bird rose up to fly away. "I did not pluck the beautiful feathers from the tails of living birds when I had the chance, so now I shall be happy to make my headdress from the splendid eagle feathers that I see lying all about me. I know now that it is wiser to take advantage of opportunities as they offer themselves."

The Boy Who Made a Snake
Mexico

Once upon a time, in a small Mexican village, there lived a poor old widow with just one son. Like many mothers, she thought that Pablo was the best boy in the whole world. She cooked and sewed for him. She washed and cleaned for him. In fact, she did all the things that he should have been doing for himself. But whenever she asked him to do the smallest thing for her, he would immediately think of a reason why he couldn't possibly do it.

Now the spring where the widow got her water every day was quite far away. The water jars were heavy, and the woman was not very strong.

"Son," she would say, "would you mind taking just a moment to go fetch me a jar of water?"

Pablo would pick up the jar and carry it away, but soon he would rush back, crying, "Mother, Mother, there was a big snake in the spring! It tried to bite me, so I ran away."

This happened so many times that the mother became very worried. Finally she said, "You had better not go near the spring anymore. It is quite clear that the snake wishes to bite only you, for it is never around when *I* dip a jar into the water."

The son was only too happy to agree. "I promise never to go near the spring again," he said.

One day, however, a friend of Pablo's came by with two empty water jars—one on each shoulder. "Would you help me?" he asked. "After I fill the jars with water I have trouble getting them on and off my shoulders."

Pablo was delighted to go along with his friend, so together they walked toward the spring. Of course, Pablo didn't worry about his mother's warning. After all, the snake was only something he had made up to get out of work. Imagine his horror, then—as he drew near the spring—to see a huge snake rise slowly to the surface of the water. Its tongue flicked in and out of its mouth like red lightning.

Pablo let out a scream and fled. But when he looked back over his shoulder, he discovered that the snake was following him.

On and on he ran, faster and faster, until he met an old donkey.
"Old donkey," he cried, "please carry me away! That big snake is
chasing me."

"When I was young and strong," said the donkey, "I worked hard
for my master. Then I grew old and weak, and he turned me out to
starve. Your mother has always worked hard for you, but you have
never made any effort to help her. So now you can help yourself for
all I care. Just keep on running!"

A little farther on, Pablo came to a skinny old horse. "Old horse," he cried, "please carry me away! That big snake is chasing me."

"When I was young and strong," said the horse, "I worked hard for my master. Then I grew old and weak, and he turned me out to starve. Your mother has always worked hard for you, but you have never made any effort to help her. So now you can help yourself for all I care. Just keep on running!"

Farther on, Pablo came to an old bull. "Old bull," he shouted, "please stand between me and that snake. Use your horns to save me."

"When I was young and strong," said the bull, "I worked hard for my master. Then I grew old and weak, and he turned me out to starve. Your mother has always worked hard for you, but you have never made any effort to help her. So now you can help yourself for all I care. Just keep on running!"

By this time Pablo was so discouraged that he sat down on a rock and began to cry. "Whatever shall I do?" he moaned.

Just then an eagle flew onto a tree limb overhead. "Why are you crying?" asked the eagle.

"Because of that snake," said the boy.

"What snake? Where?" asked the eagle.

"Crawling out of the spring," replied the boy.

"Who put it there?" asked the eagle.

"I did," Pablo admitted. "Whenever my mother sent me to fetch water, I told her a snake was there waiting to bite me."

"That was a foolish thing to do," said the eagle. "Because you kept saying, 'There is a snake in the spring,' you put one there. Such snakes are spirit snakes. The only thing to do now is to run home and tell your mother there is no snake in the spring. You put it there yourself. If she believes you, the snake will disappear."

Pablo ran home as fast as he could. "Oh, Mother," he said, "there is no snake in the spring. I told you a lie. Give me one of your water jars and I will get some water for you. You have been so good to me always. Now I want to try to help you."

His mother handed him a jar, smiling warmly.

When the boy reached the spring, he got down on his knees and stared at the clear water before dipping in his jar. The white sand bubbled on the bottom, making the reflection of a long, dark tree limb overhead ripple like the body of a snake.

"I am glad that the spirit snake is dead," said the boy. "I will do my best never to bring it back to life."

From that day on, Pablo was as good as his word. He helped his mother as much as he could, feeling grateful that she had taken such good care of him while he was young.

The Wonderful Pear Tree
China

Once upon a time, in an ancient Chinese village, a fruit peddler by the name of Wang Fu came to market with a cart full of pears. Wang Fu was a stingy old miser who always charged a high price for his pears. Nevertheless a large crowd immediately gathered around him because his pears were well known for being extra large and delicious. They came from a pear tree which grew in the blessed Valley of Chances.

As Wang Fu set his long, wooden staff to one side, an old priest pushed to the front of the crowd. There was something a little odd about this man. Although his gown looked ragged and worn, his eyes were brighter and his face finer than any others around him.

"Oh, worthy fruit peddler," said the old priest, "I am extremely hungry, for I have not eaten in a long time. Would you kindly give me one of your pears? I have no money so I cannot pay you for it. But I will bless you for your kindness."

"Be gone, you old beggar!" cried Wang Fu. "My pears are for sale. I cannot give them away. How would I make any money?"

"But you have a hundred pears in that cart," said the priest. "I am asking for only one. You would not even miss it."

"He is quite right," someone in the crowd spoke up. "Give the old man a pear. You would never miss it."

At that, other people began shouting. Some took the side of the old man; others favored the fruit peddler.

Finally the superintendent of the market heard the hubbub and came rushing up. When he made out what the trouble was, he took a coin from his own purse, bought a pear, and handed it to the priest.

"Eat it in good health, sir," he said.

The old priest bowed low before the official. Then he held the pear up in front of the crowd, saying, "Because I am a holy man, I have nothing of my own. I gave up everything to become a priest. Therefore I am deeply puzzled. Why should this peddler, who has so many good things, refuse to give me a single pear?

"I am not like that," he continued. "I have a whole tree full of wonderful pears, which I would be honored to share with you."

"If you have so many pears, old man, why are you begging for one?" asked a bystander.

"Ah," answered the priest. "First I have to grow them."

Quickly he ate the pear he was holding in his hand, saving a single small seed from the core. While the crowd watched, he took a small pick from his bag, dug a hole, and planted the seed.

"Now," he asked, "will one of you fetch me some hot water to pour on this and make it grow?"

The people in the crowd began to laugh, for they thought the old priest must be joking. But one young boy ran off to fetch a kettle of hot water. The old priest carefully poured it over the spot where he had buried the seed.

Before he had even finished pouring, the crowd saw a tiny green sprout push out of the ground. Then came another and another. The shoots kept growing taller and taller until, there before them, stood a fine young pear tree bearing first a few branches, then a few leaves. Next came more leaves, then flowers, and—last of all—clusters of huge, ripe, sweet-smelling pears.

The crowd all clapped their hands in delight. As for the priest, he began picking the pears and handing them out with a low bow to all the spectators. The selfish peddler could not believe his eyes!

When the priest had handed out the last pear, he took up his pick again and hacked at the tree until it fell with a crash. Putting it on his shoulder—leaves and all—he bowed to the bystanders and walked off.

Like everybody else, Wang Fu stared at the old priest until he had vanished from sight. Then he turned back to his own cart. To his horror he saw that it was completely empty! Every single one of his hundred pears was gone. The pears that the old priest had given away must have come from his cart. But how could that be?

Then Wang Fu discovered that his long, wooden staff was missing. There was no doubt in his mind that the priest had taken it. In a furious rage he rushed as fast as he could after the old man.

But when Wang Fu turned the corner, he discovered his staff lying close to the wall of the marketplace. One end of the stout pole looked as though someone had been hacking at it with a pick. A few leaves were lying nearby. Without any doubt his staff had been the trunk of the magical pear tree the old man had chopped down!

"Woe is me!" cried Wang Fu. "Even while I looked on, this rascal of a priest turned my staff into a tree from which he plucked my own pears to give to anyone who reached forth a hand to him."

"And it serves you right," said a farmer at his shoulder. "For only to him who freely gives does the pear tree from the Valley of Chances bear lasting fruit. Your own selfishness has given your precious pears away. This should teach you a lesson."

As for the old priest, no one ever saw him again. But those who had seen him knew that he must have been something more than a simple country priest. Very likely he had been sent by the great spirit of the misty Valley of Chances.

How There Came To Be Anansi Stories
West Africa

Long ago, in the western part of Africa, the storytellers told all their tales about Nyankupon, chief of the gods. This made Spider, who was also called Anansi, very jealous. One day he went to Nyankupon and asked if, in the future, all the tales might be about himself—Anansi. This was a bold thing to ask, but Anansi had a high opinion of himself.

Surprisingly, Nyankupon agreed—but only on one condition. Anansi must bring him three things. The first was a jar of live bees. The second was a boa constrictor, a very dangerous snake. The third was a tiger. Anansi bragged that he would soon return with all three.

First he took an earthen vessel and set out for the bees' home. As soon as he came within sight of it, he began muttering: "They will not be able to fill this jar. . . . Yes, they will. . . . No, they won't," and so on.

Finally the bees flew up to him. "What in the world are you talking about, Mr. Anansi?" they asked.

"Oh, Nyankupon insists that you will never be able to fly into this jar, and I say that you can."

"Well, of course we can," declared the bees. And in they flew, pushing and buzzing about. When the jar was full, Anansi put the cover on, and a messenger carried it to Nyankupon.

The next day Anansi took a long stick and set out to look for a boa constrictor. When he arrived at the place where one lived, he began muttering again: "He will be about as long as this stick. . . . No, he won't. . . . Yes, he will," and so on until the boa came out and asked him what was the matter.

"Oh, Nyankupon says you are not as long as this stick. I say you are. Just let me measure you and I can settle the argument." Not suspecting any trick, the boa stretched himself out straight upon the stick. The crafty Anansi lost no time in tying him to the stick from end to end. He then sent the boa constrictor to Nyankupon.

The third day he took a needle and thread and sewed up his eye. Then he set out for a den where a fierce tiger lived. As he drew near, he began to shout and sing so loudly that the tiger came out.

"My eye is sewn up," said Anansi, "and now I see such wonderful, amazing things that I cannot keep from singing about them."

"I wish you would sew up both of my eyes," said Tiger. "Then I will be able to see even more amazing sights."

Anansi immediately did so. Then, having made the tiger blind and helpless, he led him straight to the house of Nyankupon.

Nyankupon was amazed at the cleverness Anansi had shown. In fact, he was so impressed that he immediately gave the order that in the future all storytellers should call their tales—both old and new— Anansi tales. And the hero of the stories was always to be Anansi.